# THE NURSERY

# Storybook

Georgie Adams *Illustrated by* Peter Utton

Orion
Children's Books

*For Makeda, Ben, Josephine and Julia - G.A.*

*To Mike and Vera - P.U.*

First published in Great Britain in 1996
by Orion Children's Books
a division of the Orion Publishing Group Ltd
Orion House
5 Upper St Martin's Lane
London WC2H 9EA

Text copyright © Georgie Adams 1996
Illustrations copyright © Peter Utton 1996
Designed by Ian Butterworth

Georgie Adams and Peter Utton have asserted their right to be identified
as the author and illustrator of this work.

A catalogue record for this book is available from the British Library

Printed in Italy
ISBN 1 85881 230 5

# Contents

# Little Red Riding Hood

Along time ago there was a little girl called Little Red Riding Hood. For her birthday her kind old grandma had made her a cloak with a hood, all in red, and Little Red Riding Hood loved it. It was the best cloak she'd ever had. Little Red Riding Hood wore it everywhere.

One day Little Red Riding Hood's mother said, "I want you to take some cakes to Grandma. She's not very well."

Little Red Riding Hood put on her cloak and got ready at once. She packed some cakes in a basket for Grandma, slipped one in for herself and kissed her mother goodbye.

"Hurry there and back," said her mother, "and be home before dark."

Grandma lived in a village on the other side of the woods. It was a sunny day and Little Red Riding Hood skipped along a path, munching her cake. She hadn't gone far when she saw a woodcutter, chopping wood. The woodcutter stopped and waved.

"I'm going to see my grandma," said Little Red Riding Hood, through a mouthful of crumbs.

"Well, take care," said the woodcutter. "I've heard there's a wolf about who eats people. And he's always hungry!"

Little Red Riding Hood hurried on her way. The thought of meeting that wicked wolf was scary.

She had just reached the middle of the wood when a wolf popped his head round a tree. He grinned a toothy grin and licked his lips.

"I suppose you're the hungry
wolf the woodcutter told me about?"
said Little Red Riding Hood nervously.

The wolf could have gobbled up Little Red Riding Hood in one
gulp. He hadn't eaten for days. But he could hear the woodcutter at
work nearby and thought better of it.

So the wolf said he wasn't in the least bit interested in lunch
(wolves will lie through their teeth when it suits them!) and
Little Red Riding Hood believed him.

"Where are you off to?" asked the wolf.

"I'm going to see my grandma," replied Little Red Riding Hood. "I'm taking her some cakes."

The wolf pricked up his ears. He had heard that grandmas were good to eat. Here was his chance to try one.

"Where does she live?" he said.

"Over there," said Little Red Riding Hood. "Through the trees, down the lane, first cottage by the mill."

By this time the wolf's tummy was gurgling like a drain. He thought of a cunning plan to eat Grandma *and* Little Red Riding Hood. You see how greedy he was!

"I'll go and see her, too," said the wolf. "I'll walk this way, you go that, and we'll see who gets there first."

So Little Red Riding Hood set off again, and on the way she stopped to pick some flowers.

Now, as you may have guessed, the wolf chose the shortest path to Grandma's place. He had sent Little Red Riding Hood round the long way. The wolf strolled along for the first few paces until the little girl was out of sight. Then he ran flat out through the woods and arrived at the cottage before her.

The wolf knocked on the door.

"Who's there?" called Grandma from the bedroom.

"It's me, Little Red Riding Hood," said the wolf, in a voice which he hoped sounded like Little Red Riding Hood's. "I've brought you some cakes."

"Ooo, lovely!" said Grandma. "Just what I fancy. Open the door, wipe your feet and come in."

So the wolf went in and, finding
Grandma tucked up in bed and ready
to eat, he sprang . . . and swallowed
her up in one go.

"Ugh!" cried Grandma as she
slid past his tonsils and into his
stomach. "It's dark down here."

The wolf patted his tummy. All that
was left of Grandma was her nightcap.
It was woolly and tickled his throat.

Well, that was bad enough, but as you know the wolf planned to wait for Little Red Riding Hood and eat her, too. So he wriggled into Grandma's spare nightdress, put on her nightcap and climbed into bed.

Little Red Riding Hood will think I'm her grandma, he thought, as he pulled the blankets up to his chin.

The wolf didn't have to wait long before there was a *tap-tap-tap* at the door.

"Who's there?" he called.

"It's me, Little Red Riding Hood," said Little Red Riding Hood. "I've brought you some cakes."

"Ooo, lovely!" said the wolf. "You're . . . I mean, *they're* just what I fancy. Open the door, wipe your feet and . . . COME IN."

Little Red Riding Hood thought her grandma's voice sounded a little gruffer than usual. I expect that's because she's not very well, thought Little Red Riding Hood as she stepped inside . . .

Little Red Riding Hood went to her grandma's bedside and got quite a shock. Her grandma didn't look herself at all.

"Put your basket down, my dear," said the wolf, "and sit by me." He patted the bed with his paw.

"Grandma, what big, hairy arms you have!" said Little Red Riding Hood.

"All the better to *hug* you with, my dear," said the wolf, giving her plump little hand a squeeze.

"But Grandma, what big ears you have!"

"All the better to *hear* you with, my dear," said the wolf, waggling both ears at once.

Then Little Red Riding Hood said,
"But Grandma, what big eyes you have!"
"All the better to *see* you with, my
dear," said the wolf, swivelling his
eyeballs and grinning from ear to ear.

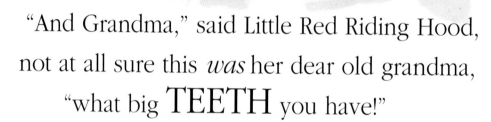

"And Grandma," said Little Red Riding Hood,
not at all sure this *was* her dear old grandma,
"what big TEETH you have!"
"All the better to EAT you with, my
dear!" said the wolf with a wicked
laugh. And he leaped out of bed.
Little Red Riding Hood screamed and
ran out of the cottage, yelling

for help. The wolf tried to chase after her but
he tripped on Grandma's
nightdress and the
woolly nightcap
slipped over his
eyes. He couldn't
see a thing.

Luckily, the woodcutter was on his way home for tea and heard Little Red Riding Hood shouting.

He rushed into the cottage and the wolf bumped straight into him.

"Got you!" said the woodcutter.

And he chopped him down dead.

"I think he's eaten my grandma," sobbed Little Red Riding Hood. "Look, there's something moving inside!"

So the woodcutter carefully cut the wolf down the middle and out stepped Grandma. The greedy wolf had swallowed her whole.

Grandma was a bit upset, but not for long.

"Now, where are those cakes?" she said.

So they each had a cake from Little Red Riding Hood's basket, which made them feel much better.

Grandma thanked the woodcutter for his help. Then Little Red Riding Hood kissed her grandma goodbye and the woodcutter took her home.

And from that day on, Little Red Riding Hood always ran through the woods without stopping and never spoke to a wolf again!

# The Elves and the Shoemaker

There was once a shoemaker called Mr Slipper who was brilliant at making shoes. Boots with buckles; shoes with bows; high heels, low heels, no heels . . . he could make them all. There wasn't a foot he couldn't fit.

The only trouble was, not enough people came into Mr Slipper's shop to buy shoes, and he and his wife were very poor.

To make matters worse, there came a day when Mr Slipper had just enough leather to make one more pair of shoes. That evening he cut out the leather and began to nail the heels with his hammer.

But the hammer slipped and . . . *Bang!*
"Ouch!" cried Mr Slipper, as he missed
the nail and hit his thumb instead. It
was tingling painfully.

"There, there!" said Mrs Slipper,
bandaging his sore thumb. "Go to bed
and finish those shoes in the morning."

But next morning after breakfast, when
Mr Slipper went to work . . . there, on the table was the finest pair of
shoes he had ever seen. They were a surprise, I can tell you.

Mr Slipper examined the shoes closely. The stitches were neat.
The heels were trimmed. And the leather was so beautifully polished,
he could see his face in the toes.

Mr Slipper showed them to his wife.

"Quick!" she said. "Put them in the shop window."

Well, just then a man walked by and saw the shoes.

"At last!" he exclaimed. "I've been looking for a pair like that for weeks."

The man was so pleased with the shoes, he gave Mr Slipper a purse full of silver and left the shop wearing them.

Mr Slipper counted the coins. Now he had enough money to buy leather for *two* pairs of shoes.

That evening the shoemaker cut out the leather, and began to nail the heels. But holding the nail wasn't easy with his sore thumb and . . .

*Bang! Bang!* "Ouch! Ouch!" cried Mr Slipper as he missed the nail and hit two fingers at once.

"There, there!" said Mrs Slipper, getting out the first-aid box again. "Go to bed and finish those shoes in the morning."

And guess what? When Mr Slipper started work the next morning, he found two pairs of shoes ready to sell. He could hardly believe his eyes.

The shoemaker put both pairs in the shop, and very soon two rich ladies came and bought them. They each gave Mr Slipper a bag of silver - enough to buy leather for *six* pairs of shoes!

That evening Mr Slipper cut out the leather. But when he went to nail the heels . . . Mrs Slipper said,

"Stop! Let's wait up tonight and see who has been making all these shoes. Besides . . ." she added, removing the hammer, "I'm running out of bandages."

So Mr Slipper and his wife hid behind a
cupboard and waited. All was quiet in the
workshop until, on the stroke of midnight,
there was a scuttling sound. Mr and Mrs
Slipper peered down. There, creeping
across the floor, were two little men in tatty
torn trousers and threadbare coats.
"Elves!" gasped Mr and Mrs Slipper together.
And so they were.

The shoemaker and his wife watched wide-eyed as the elves clambered on to the table, opened bags of tiny tools and set to work. Nimble fingers snipped and stitched.

And as they worked, they sang a song:

*"Heels and toes,*
*Laces and bows.*
*Nobody knows*
*Who shapes and sews*
*Shoes so neat*
*For big folks' feet!"*

And believe it or not, before the clock struck one, those elves had made six pairs of shiny new shoes. Six pairs in an hour! You try it. It's impossible. Then before Mr Slipper or his wife could utter a word, the little men packed up their tools and scampered away.

"Well, I never!" said Mr Slipper. "Those shoes will fetch a lot of money."

"We must thank the elves," said Mrs Slipper. "But how?"

Mr Slipper thought for a moment.

"They were thinly dressed . . ." he began.

"Then we'll make them warm clothes!" said his wife.

Mrs Slipper got up early in the morning and was soon busy with scissors, thread and scraps of material. First she sewed two teeny shirts, with weeny buttons, collars and cuffs. Then she cut out two pairs of trousers, thick jackets and waistcoats. And while she was sewing, her husband made the tiniest boots you have ever seen. By evening, the clothes were ready.

Mr and Mrs Slipper left everything in the workshop and hid behind the cupboard. Sure enough, at midnight, the elves came creeping in. But, instead of shoe leather, they found two tidy piles of new clothes.

The little men threw off their shabby rags and put on the outfits with great excitement. The shirts, trousers, waistcoats and jackets were all beautifully made and just the right size. Last of all they pulled on the tiny boots and danced a jig on the table.

The shoemaker and his wife smiled to see them so happy. They listened as the elves sang this song:

*"Warm new clothes*
*From head to toes.*
*What a treat!*
*We're dressed so neat.*
*No need to cobble*
*big folks' feet."*

And that was that. In two blinks the elves had gone and were never seen again. But the shoemaker and his wife didn't mind.

From that day on, Mr Slipper's shop was always full of customers and they lived comfortably for the rest of their days.

# The Three Billy-Goats Gruff

There were once three billy-goats called Little Billy-Goat Gruff, Middle Billy-Goat Gruff and Big Billy-Goat Gruff and they all lived together on the side of a mountain.

Little Billy-Goat Gruff was the smallest
of the three. He was snowy white with
two little horns, spriggy as twigs.

Middle Billy-Goat Gruff was
neither big nor little; just middling
size, with nimble legs and soft
brown eyes.

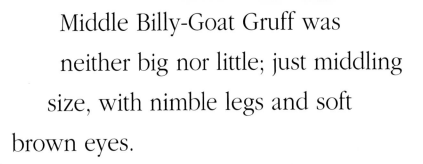

But Big Billy-Goat Gruff
wasn't called Big for
nothing. He was enormous!
Big Billy-Goat Gruff had two
terrible horns like battering
rams, and he could butt like
a bulldozer.

One day the three billy-goats looked across
the river at the foot of the mountain. The long
green grass that grew on the
other side looked much
tastier to eat. But to get there they had
to go over a bridge.

Now under the bridge lived a troll.
Trolls are never nice, and this one was mean

and smelly, with hairy feet and skinny arms. He had eyes as big as dinner plates and a long warty nose that twitched when he was angry. The nasty troll guarded the bridge day and night and never, EVER let anyone cross it.

The billy-goats knew all about the troll, but the grass looked so good they just *had* to get to the other side. So they thought of a plan to trick that mean old troll.

First came Little Billy-Goat Gruff with his horns as spriggy as twigs. His little hooves went *trip-trap, trip-trap* over the bridge. When he was halfway across, the troll popped his head out and roared,

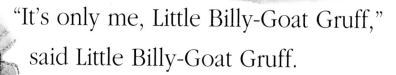

"Who's that trip-trapping over my bridge?"

"It's only me, Little Billy-Goat Gruff," said Little Billy-Goat Gruff.

"Well, I'm going to eat you up!" said the troll.

You see how horrible he was.

"Oh, no!" said Little Billy-Goat Gruff. "I'm too little. Wait until Middle Billy-Goat Gruff comes along. He's much bigger."

The troll scratched his ear and thought about it. He had never, EVER let anyone cross before, but the bigger billy-goat *would* make a better meal.

"All right," said the greedy troll. "Be off with you!"

So Little Billy-Goat Gruff crossed over the bridge to the other side.

In a while Middle Billy-Goat Gruff came along with his nimble legs and soft brown eyes. His middling hooves went *TRIP-TRAP, TRIP-TRAP* over the bridge. When he was halfway across, that bad-tempered troll popped his head out and roared,

"Who's that trip-trapping over my bridge?"

"It's only me, Middle Billy-Goat Gruff," said Middle Billy-Goat Gruff.

"Well, I'm going to eat you up!" said the troll.

"Oh, please don't do that," said Middle Billy-Goat Gruff. "I'm not very big. Wait until Big Billy-Goat Gruff comes along. He's much bigger!"

The troll stamped his hairy feet and snorted. He had only EVER let one billy-goat cross before, but if there was a bigger one right behind . . .

"All right," said the greedy troll. "Be off with you!"

So Middle Billy-Goat Gruff crossed over the bridge, too.

Sure enough, Big Billy-Goat Gruff did come along with his two terrible horns like battering rams. His heavy hooves went *TRIP-TRAP! TRIP-TRAP!* over the bridge, and made such a noise. When he was halfway across, that hairy old troll popped his head out and roared,

"Who's that TRIP-TRAPPING over my bridge?"

The troll was so angry that his eyes spun round like cartwheels and his nose twitched up and down.

"It's me, Big Billy-Goat Gruff," boomed Big Billy-Goat Gruff in the loudest, gruffest voice you have ever heard. It rumbled round the mountain like thunder.

"Well, I'm going to eat you up!" said the troll.

"Ha! Just you try!" roared Big Billy-Goat Gruff.

Well, the foolish troll climbed on to the bridge, hopping mad. But that didn't worry Big Billy-Goat Gruff. Oh no. Big Billy-Goat Gruff snorted, put his head down and . . . . .
CHARGED!

He butted that troll so hard, the troll flew up in the air and over the mountain, and was never seen again.

Then Big Billy-Goat Gruff crossed over the bridge and joined Little Billy-Goat Gruff and Middle Billy-Goat Gruff on the other side. They ate the long green grass and grew so fat they could hardly walk home.

# The Real Princess

There was once a prince who wanted to marry a princess. Nothing very unusual about that. Only she had to be a *real* princess, and finding one wasn't easy.

The prince travelled all over the world searching for a wife. He went to one palace after another and met lots of girls who *said* they were princesses. They all wore silk dresses and diamond tiaras, but the prince could never be sure if the princesses were real or not.

So the prince returned home feeling miserable.

The king and queen weren't too happy about it, either. They wished their son would hurry up and marry. Then he could rule the country and they could go on holiday!

As luck would have it, there *was* a princess (a real princess) who lived just down the road. She didn't live in a palace or wear fine dresses. In fact, she lived over a grocer's shop with Their Majesties, her mum and dad.

Her parents *had* been king and queen of the land next-door, but the Royal Treasurer had run off with all their money. So they had to sell the palace and move.

Now the real princess
thought she would like to marry the prince. So one day she set off
for the palace. On the way there was a terrible storm, with thunder
and lightning. Rain poured from the sky and the real princess got
drenched. Water dripped down her hair as she knocked at the
palace door.

The king opened it and found the princess standing on the
doorstep. What with the wind and the rain, she looked a mess.

The poor girl was soaking wet and her toes squelched inside her shoes. But she said she was a real princess.

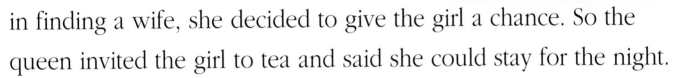

The prince's mother didn't believe her for a minute, but since the prince hadn't had much luck in finding a wife, she decided to give the girl a chance. So the queen invited the girl to tea and said she could stay for the night.

While the real princess toasted her toes by the fire and ate delicious cream cakes, the queen slipped upstairs to the spare bedroom. She had thought of a way to find out if the girl really *was* a princess.

First the queen took the bedclothes off the bed and laid one hard little pea on the bedstead.

Then she heaved twenty mattresses on to the bed and piled them one on top of the other. And, as if that wasn't enough, she took twenty feather eiderdowns and put those on top of the mattresses!

And that is where the princess was to sleep that night.

The next morning the queen asked her how she had slept.

The princess complained, bitterly. "I've had a terrible night," she said. "I've hardly slept a wink. Goodness knows what was in the bed. I felt something hard and it has bruised me all over!"

Well, that proved it. The queen saw at once that the girl must be a real princess. She had felt one little pea through twenty mattresses and twenty feather eiderdowns. Only a real princess could be so delicate.

So the prince asked the real princess to marry him and the real princess said,

"Yes, as long as I don't have to sleep in that bed again."
After the wedding, the king and queen invited the princess's mum and dad to come and live in the palace. And every year, Their Majesties all went on holiday to the seaside. So everyone was happy.

Now that's a *real* story, isn't it?

# The Gingerbread Man

This is a story about a little old man and a little old woman, who lived together in a little old house. They had no children of their own, and sometimes the little old man and the little old woman were sad about that.

One day the little old woman made a man out of gingerbread. She mixed up the dough, squashed him into shape and cut out a jacket and cap. Then the little old woman gave him two currant eyes and a nut for a nose and popped him in the oven.

In a while the little old woman said to herself,
"That gingerbread man must be ready by now."
And she opened the oven door.

Well, to her surprise, the gingerbread man
jumped up on his bendy legs . . . and ran out
of the house!

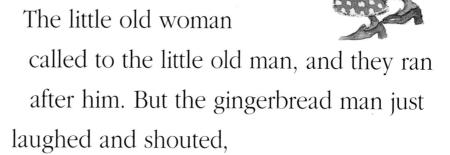

The little old woman
called to the little old man, and they ran
after him. But the gingerbread man just
laughed and shouted,

*"Run, run, as fast as you can.*
*You can't catch me,*
*I'm the gingerbread man!"*

The little old woman and the little
old man ran as fast as they could, but
they couldn't catch him.

The gingerbread man ran on, until he
came to a cow, grazing in a field.

"Stop!" said the cow. "You look good
enough to eat."

The gingerbread man only laughed and said,

*"I have run away from a little old woman
and a little old man
and I can run away from you, I can!*

*Run, run, as fast as you can.
You can't catch me,
I'm the gingerbread man!"*

And the cow couldn't catch him.

The gingerbread man ran on
until he came to a horse, eating hay.
The horse thought, Hm! that gingerbread
man looks delicious!

"Please stop," said the horse.

But the gingerbread man didn't do any such thing. He just ran
on shouting,

*"I have run away from a little old woman,*
*a little old man*
*and a cow*
*and I can run away from you, I can!*

*Run, run, as fast as you can.*
*You can't catch me,*
*I'm the gingerbread man!"*

The horse gave chase, but he couldn't catch him.

Soon after that, the gingerbread man
ran past some children playing in the park. The
children were very hungry.

"Stop!" cried the children. "We want to eat you."

But the gingerbread man didn't stop. He ran by the children
shouting,

"*I have run away from a little old woman,*
*a little old man,*
*a cow*
*and a horse*
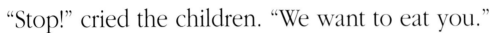
*and I can run away from you, I can!*

*Run, run, as fast as you can.*
*You can't catch me,*
*I'm the gingerbread man!*"

Then the children left the park and ran after
the gingerbread man. But they couldn't catch him.

Now by this time the gingerbread man
was so pleased with himself, he didn't think
anyone could catch him. He ran like the
wind until . . . he came to a river.

And stopped.

The gingerbread man couldn't swim and
the little old woman and the little old man, the
cow, the horse and all the children were still chasing him.

Just then a fox came by. The
gingerbread man was worried, but he
sang out all the same,

*"I have run away from a little old woman,*
*a little old man,*
*a cow,*
*a horse*
*and a park full of children*
*and I can run away from you, I can!*

*Run, run, as fast as you can.*
*You can't catch me,*
*I'm the gingerbread man!"*

The clever fox thought the gingerbread man would make a tasty snack, but he pretended not to care.

"I wouldn't catch you, even if I could," said the fox. "But I'll help you across the river."

The gingerbread man could see the others coming. He hadn't a moment to lose.

"Hop on to my tail," said the fox. "And we'll be off!"

So the gingerbread man hopped on to the fox's tail and the fox began to swim. They had gone only a little way, when the fox said,

"The water is getting deeper. Climb on my back, so you won't get wet."

So the gingerbread man climbed on his back.

In the middle of the river the fox said,

"The water is even deeper. Climb on my head, so you won't get wet."

So the gingerbread man climbed on his head.

Then the fox said,

"The water is up to my neck! Climb on my nose, so you won't get wet."

So the gingerbread man climbed on to the very tip of his nose. And the crafty fox threw back his head and . . . caught the gingerbread man between his teeth.

"Oh, my!" said the gingerbread man.

*snap!*

And after that . . . the gingerbread man never said another word.

# Goldilocks and the Three Bears

Once upon a time there were three bears, who lived in a neat and tidy house in the woods.

Father Bear was a great big bear.

Mother Bear was a middle-sized bear.

And Baby Bear was a small wee bear.

The three bears were very well-behaved and never did any harm.

One day Mother Bear made hot porridge
for breakfast, and poured it into three
bowls. There was a great big bowl
for Father Bear, a middle-sized bowl
for Mother Bear, and a tiny little
bowl for Baby Bear.

Then, because they were sensible
bears, they left their porridge to cool and
went for a walk.

While they were out, a little girl called Goldilocks came along. She was supposed to be doing some shopping for her mother, but when she saw the house she forgot all about that and walked up the garden path.

Goldilocks looked through the window - nosy girl! Worse still, she peeped through the keyhole and, seeing no one about she opened the door and walked in.

Goldilocks had a good look round. She saw the porridge on the table and, as bold as you like, she helped herself.

First Goldilocks tasted the porridge in Father Bear's bowl, but that was too hot. Then she tried the porridge in Mother Bear's bowl, but that was too cold. And then she tasted the porridge in Baby Bear's bowl and that was just right! So she ate it all up.

With her tummy full of porridge, Goldilocks felt a bit sick, and she looked for somewhere to sit. First she sat in Father Bear's chair, but that was too high. Then she sat in Mother Bear's chair, but that was too wide. And then she saw Baby Bear's chair and that seemed just right! So she plonked herself down on it, but the little chair fell to pieces.

"Bother!" said Goldilocks crossly, and wasn't at all sorry she had broken it.

By this time Goldilocks was feeling sleepy and she went upstairs to the bedroom.

First she lay on Father Bear's bed, but that was too hard.

Then she lay on Mother Bear's bed, but that was too soft.

And then she lay on Baby Bear's bed and that was just right! So she snuggled under the blankets (without bothering to take her shoes off) and fell asleep.

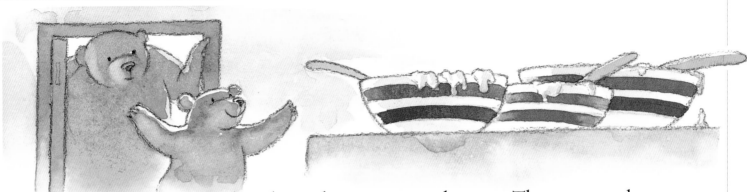

At that moment the three bears came home. They were hungry and looking forward to eating their porridge. But oh, dear! Goldilocks had carelessly left the spoons standing in the bowls.

**"SOMEBODY HAS BEEN EATING MY PORRIDGE!"**
said Father Bear, in his deep growly voice.

"SOMEBODY HAS BEEN EATING MY PORRIDGE!" said Mother Bear, in her middling growly voice.

"SOMEBODY HAS BEEN EATING MY PORRIDGE!" said Baby Bear, in his small wee voice. "AND THEY'VE EATEN IT ALL UP!"

The three bears were sure someone had been in their house so they looked around. Now because they were neat and tidy bears, they always left the cushions straight in the chairs. But oh, dear! Goldilocks hadn't bothered to do that and the bears were quick to notice.

**"SOMEBODY HAS BEEN SITTING IN MY CHAIR!"**
said Father Bear, in his deep growly voice.

"SOMEBODY HAS BEEN SITTING IN MY CHAIR!" said Mother Bear, in her middling growly voice.

"SOMEBODY HAS BEEN SITTING IN MY CHAIR!"
said Baby Bear, in his small wee voice.
"AND THEY'VE BROKEN IT!"

Just then the three bears heard a sound coming from the bedroom. It was Goldilocks snoring. So the three bears padded upstairs, to see what was going on.

The bears always made their beds in the morning and smoothed the covers straight. But oh, dear! Goldilocks had messed them up.

**"SOMEBODY HAS BEEN LYING IN MY BED!"**

said Father Bear, in his deep growly voice.

"SOMEBODY HAS BEEN LYING IN MY BED!" said Mother Bear, in her middling growly voice.

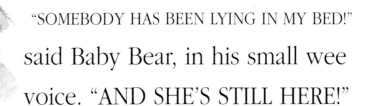

"SOMEBODY HAS BEEN LYING IN MY BED!" said Baby Bear, in his small wee voice. "AND SHE'S STILL HERE!"

The sound of Baby Bear's high voice pinged like an alarm
clock in Goldilock's ear. She peered over the covers and saw

great big Father Bear and
middle-sized Mother Bear and
small wee Baby Bear - all staring at her.

Goldilocks got such a fright that she
leaped out of bed, slid down the banisters
and ran all the way home to her mother.
  And that wasn't all. Goldilocks was
sent to bed without any supper for not
doing the shopping.
  Which served her right.

# The Three Little Pigs

This is a story of three little pigs.
One day their mother said,
"You've all grown into fine little pigs.
Now it's time for you to make homes
of your own."

Mrs Pig packed some food and kissed
each little pig on the nose.

"Take care!" warned Mrs Pig. "There's a big bad wolf about.
Build your houses good and strong, and NEVER let that bad old
wolf through the door."

So the three little pigs said goodbye and went on their way.

The first little pig strolled down the road. He couldn't be bothered to walk very far, and the thought of building a house made him tired. Besides, he had nothing to build it with. So he sat down in the sun and ate his sandwiches.

In a while a farmer came along with some straw.

Just what I need! thought the first little pig. So he said to the farmer, "Will you give me some straw to build a house?"

The farmer had plenty, so he gave the little pig a big bundle. The little pig thanked the farmer and made a house of straw.

He was just settling himself inside, when that big bad wolf his mother had warned him about came along. The clever wolf had sniffed the little pig a mile away. He licked his lips, smiled and (this is the crafty bit) knocked on the door.

"Little pig, little pig, let me come in," said the wolf.

The first little pig was lazy, but he wasn't silly, so he replied, "No! Not by the hair of my chinny, chin chin."

"Then I'll huff and I'll puff and I'll blow your house in!" said the wolf.

So he huffed and he puffed and he blew the house in and ate up the first little pig.

The second little pig went into the forest. He plodded along, grumbling about this and that, as grumpy piggies do. He grumbled most about having to build his own house. Besides, he had nothing to build it with.

He hadn't gone far when he met some campers collecting sticks for their fire. Just what I need! thought the second little pig. So he said to the campers,

"Will you give me some sticks to build a house?" The campers had plenty of sticks, so they gave the little pig enough to build a house. The little pig cheered up a bit after that, thanked the campers and built a house of sticks.

He had only just finished, when the wolf came by. After the first little pig's unfortunate end, the hungry wolf had sniffed his way to the forest in search of another tasty meal.

The cunning wolf knocked on the door and said,

"Little pig, little pig, let me come in."

The second little pig was grumpy, but he wasn't silly, so he replied,

"No! Not by the hair of my chinny, chin chin."

"Then I'll huff and I'll puff and I'll blow your house in!" said the wolf.

So he huffed and he puffed, he puffed and he huffed until at last he blew the house in . . . and ate up the second little pig.

Now, the third little pig was quite different. She took the path across the fields to town and met some builders, unloading bricks.

"Please, will you give me some bricks to build a house?" said the third (and cleverest) little pig.

The builders had plenty of bricks, so they gave the little pig all she needed. The little pig thanked the builders, loaded the bricks into a cart and built herself a good, strong house. Then she went inside and shut the door.

The third little pig was just about to have tea when the wolf came along. The wolf knocked on the door and said,

"Little pig, little pig, let me come in."

But the third little pig wasn't silly at all and she replied, "No! Not by the hair of my chinny, chin chin."

"Then I'll huff and I'll puff and I'll blow your house in!" said the wolf.

Well, he huffed and he puffed. He puffed and he huffed and he huffed and puffed together, but he *could not* blow the house in.

When the wolf saw that all his huffing and puffing was getting him nowhere, he thought for a moment and said,

"Little pig, I know where there are some carrots."

"Where?" said the little pig.

"In the field by the river," said the wolf. "If you like, I'll call for you at seven o'clock tomorrow morning, and we'll go there together."

So the little pig agreed to go. But instead of waiting for the wolf to collect her at seven o'clock, the little pig went out at six o'clock and got the carrots all by herself. You see how clever she was.

When the wolf came at seven o'clock, he wasn't at all pleased to hear that the little pig had been there and back already. He had never been tricked like this before! The wolf thought for a while. Then he said,

"Little pig, I know where there is a tree full of rosy apples."

"Where?" said the little pig.

"In the farmer's orchard," said the wolf. "I'll call for you at six o'clock and we'll go there together."

So the little pig agreed to go. But instead of waiting for the wolf to collect her at six o'clock, the little pig went off to the orchard at five o'clock. She had hoped to get to the apple tree and back before the wolf arrived. But it took the little pig some time to climb the tree and she was still up there when the wolf came along.

The little pig looked down and was very frightened.

"I see you have got here before me," said the wolf. "Are they nice apples?"

"Yes," said the little pig. "Here, taste one for yourself."

The little pig threw an apple as far as she could. It landed in a muddy ditch and the wolf scrambled after it. While the

wolf was in the ditch, the little pig climbed down the tree and ran home.

By now the wolf was losing patience. The little pig had tricked him twice, but he came to the house a third time and said,

"Little pig, there is a fair in town this afternoon. Would you like to go?"

"Oh, yes," said the little pig. "What time shall I meet you there?"

"At three o'clock," said the wolf.

As usual, the little pig went earlier. She got to the fair at two o'clock and bought a butter-churn.

On the way home, the little pig saw the wolf going to the fair, so she jumped into the butter-churn to hide.

Now the churn was at the top of a hill and, as the little pig wriggled inside, it toppled over and rolled all the way down to the bottom.

When the wolf saw the
churn spinning towards him, it scared his
whiskers off! He ran for his life and forgot
all about going to the fair.

But later that day, he went to the little pig's house and knocked
on the door. The little pig still wouldn't let him in. So he called
through the keyhole and told her what had happened. The little pig
laughed and said,

"I was inside that churn."

Well, that made the wolf red hot mad, and he said,

"Little pig, little pig, you've tricked me once
over the carrots, twice over the apples and
three times over the fair. But you won't get
away from me this time. I'm coming down
the chimney to eat you up!"

The wolf climbed on to the roof of the little pig's house, and squeezed himself into the chimney. Quick as anything, the little pig took her biggest cooking pot, filled it with water and put it on the fire.

The fire blazed.

The water boiled.

The wolf came down the chimney *SPLASH!* and fell head first into the cooking pot. And that was the end of the big bad wolf!

After that, the little pig lived happily in her little brick house - and as far as I know, she lives there still.

# Jack and the Beanstalk

Once upon a time there was a poor mother who lived alone with her son, Jack. They owned a scraggy old cow called Doris, and all they had to live on was a bucketful of milk she gave each morning.

Doris did her best, but there came a time when she had no more milk to give.

"Take the cow to market and get the best price you can," said Jack's mother. "With the money she fetches, we can buy some food."

So Jack set off down the road with Doris. He hadn't walked more than a mile when he met a man.

"Where are you going?" asked the man.

"I'm off to market to sell my cow," replied Jack.

"Ha! call that a cow!" laughed the man. "You don't know how many beans make five!"

"Two in one hand, two in the other and one under your hat," said Jack, sharp as a needle. "That's how many beans make five."

"Well, you're not such a fool," said the man, taking five strange-looking beans from his pocket. "I'll tell you what. I'll give you five beans for your old cow."

"What!" said Jack. "My mother would fry my ears for supper if I went home with beans."

"Ah," said the man. "But these are *magic* beans. Plant them tonight and see what happens. Trust me, they'll bring you good luck."

So Jack sold Doris for five beans.

"You've been quick," said Jack's mother, when he got home. "How much did you get for the cow?"

"You'll never guess," said Jack.

"Ooh!" said his mother, thinking her son had struck a good bargain. "Tell me quick, I can't wait."

"Five . . . beans," said Jack.

"Beans!" shrieked his mother. "Beans! You've sold the cow for *beans*! You brainless blockhead, what good are those?"

"They're magic . . ." began Jack. But before he could get any further, his mother grabbed the beans, threw them into the garden and sent Jack to bed.

Poor Jack felt miserable. He had made a mess of things. They had no cow, no money and nothing to live on - all because he had been such a ninny.

When Jack woke the next morning, his room was unusually dark. He peered through the window, but all he could see were leaves. Bean leaves! Jack ran downstairs and went outside. The beans his mother had tossed out the night before had grown into a beanstalk. And a whopping great thing it was, too.

Jack looked up. The beanstalk went past the roof, over the treetops and through the clouds.

"So they *were* magic beans after all," Jack said to himself. "I wonder where it goes?"

There was only one way to find out. Jack clambered up that beanstalk like a monkey after nuts. It was a good long way, but at last Jack stuck his head above the clouds and reached the top.

The boy looked around and saw a path leading to a house. Mind you, it was no ordinary house. It was mind-boggling big, with a roof the size of two football pitches.

I wonder who lives here? thought Jack, as he struggled to ring the doorbell. The door was opened by an enormous woman. Jack could hardly see over her slippers.

"Good morning," said Jack politely. " Would you be kind enough to give me some breakfast?"

"If it's breakfast you want, it's breakfast you'll be, if you don't watch out," said the huge woman. "Don't you know my husband's an ogre? He eats little boys mashed on toast."

"Oh, please!" said Jack. "I've come a long way and I'm very hungry."

The ogre's wife wasn't half so bad as she looked. She took Jack into the kitchen and gave him some bread and a chunk of cheese. Then, as Jack was munching, the ogre came stomping down the garden path. Each gigantic footstep shook the house.

"Quick!" said the ogre's wife. "Jump in the oven. He'll never find you there."

As Jack crouched inside the oven, the ogre clumped into the kitchen. He was massive; twice the size of his wife with legs like tree-trunks.

The ogre sniffed and got a whiff of Jack.

*"Fee, fi, fo, fum,*
*I smell the blood of an Englishman.*
*Be he alive or be he dead,*
*I'll grind his bones to make my bread!"*

he boomed.

"Nonsense," said his wife. "It must be the cow I boiled for your breakfast. Now, sit down and eat it while it's hot."

The ogre grunted and sat down. He picked up a leg with his podgy fingers and crunched the bones. Grease dribbled down his stubbly chin and dripped all over his shirt. It was a revolting sight.

When he had finished, the ogre got up and went to a chest in the corner of the room. Jack peeped through a crack in the oven door. He saw the ogre take two bags and plonk them on the table. Then he opened each one and tipped out a great pile of coins. Gold coins!

Jack watched as the ogre counted his treasure. In a while the ogre grew sleepy and dozed off, snorting like a hundred pigs.

Jack crept out of his hiding place and shinned up a table leg. He shovelled as many coins as he could carry into a bag. Then he flung it over his shoulder and ran for his life! He sped along the path, jumped on the beanstalk and climbed down, fast.

"Mother!" shouted Jack, running into the cottage with the bag of gold.

Jack's mother was flabbergasted. "You're a brave boy," she said, "but you must promise never to climb that beanstalk again."

Well, Jack promised and for a time he and his mother lived well and had plenty of food. But money doesn't last for ever, and neither did Jack's promise. One day, when his mother wasn't looking, Jack scrambled up the beanstalk again.

He arrived on the ogre's doorstep and rang the bell. The huge woman opened the door.

"You again!" she said.

"Just passing," said Jack, with a grin. "It's a hot day and I'm thirsty."

"Hm!" said the woman. "The last time you were here, some of my husband's gold went missing."

"Really?" said Jack. "Well, my throat is so dry, I really couldn't say a word about that."

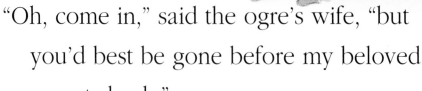

"Oh, come in," said the ogre's wife, "but you'd best be gone before my beloved gets back."

Unfortunately for Jack, her beloved returned early from hunting. Jack heard his noisy footsteps and hid himself in the oven.

*Clump! Clump! Clump!* In came the ogre with three bulls dangling from his belt.

"I'll have these roasted for dinner," he told his wife.

Then the ogre sniffed. "There's a boy in here, I'm sure of it," he growled.

*"Fee, fi, fo, fum,*
*I smell the blood of an Englishman.*
*Be he alive or be he dead,*
*I'll grind his bones to make my bread!"*

"Oh fee, fi, fiddlesticks!" said his wife. "It's probably the horse I cooked for lunch. Sit and eat it, do!"

So her husband ate his lunch, licked the plate and belched. Ogres are not particular about their table manners. Then he fetched a beautiful red hen and stroked it very gently.

"Lay, hen, lay," whispered the ogre.

The hen laid an egg - not just an ordinary egg, but one made of gold! After a few minutes the ogre felt sleepy. He sprawled in the chair and was soon snoring like thunder.

Jack saw his chance. He jumped out of the oven, snatched the hen and ran. The hen squawked, but Jack kept on running all the way to the beanstalk. He grabbed the stem with one hand and clutched the hen with the other.

When he got home, Jack said to his mother,
"Watch this."

He stroked the hen gently and whispered,
"Lay, hen, lay."

As before, the hen laid a beautiful golden egg.

Well, of course, Jack's mother was as pleased as anything, but she made Jack promise, really *promise* not to go up that beanstalk again. The golden eggs would buy all they could want for the rest of their days.

Time went by until one day, Jack was feeling bored. He had no need to work and there was nothing to do. He gazed up at the beanstalk and felt he just *had* to climb it once more. So early the next morning, while his mother was still asleep, Jack went up, hand over hand, and very soon reached the top.

Only this time, he didn't go straight to the ogre's house. Jack wasn't silly. What with the missing gold and the hen, he had a feeling the ogre's wife wouldn't let him in. So instead he hid behind a bush and waited for her to come out.

In a while, the door banged open and the huge woman came to fetch water from the well. Jack slipped inside the house and hid in a water-jar. Then, *Thump! Clump! Thump! Clump!* the ogre and his wife came into the kitchen. As the two sat down for a snack, the ogre sniffed suspiciously.

"What's the matter, dearie?" asked his wife. "Those are best pigs' trotters. Eat up. They're your favourite."

"Can't you smell it?" roared the ogre.

*"Fee, fi, fo, fum,*
*I smell the blood of an Englishman.*
*Be he alive or be he dead,*
*I'll grind his bones to make my bread!"*

He got up from the table and looked around.

"You and your fee, fi, fo, fumming," scorned the wife. "How you do go on!"

The ogre was sure he could smell a boy. He looked under the sink, in the cupboards, behind the cake tin - everwhere, except (luckily for Jack) in the water-jar.

At last the ogre gave up, finished his trotters and went to fetch his harp. It was made of gold and had a strange figure carved on one side. The ogre, who was feeling tired, slumped in a chair and said to the harp, "Play!"

Now this was a magic harp and it played and sang all by itself. It lulled the ogre to sleep.

At the first rumbling, gurgling snore Jack squeezed himself out of the water-jar. The ogre's wife was busy at the sink and didn't see him tiptoe across the floor. The golden harp was singing quietly to itself when Jack seized it from behind.

"Master! Master!" cried the harp.

Jack tried to muffle its cries with his hand. Too late! The ogre woke up and saw Jack running off with his most precious possession.

"After him!" yelled his wife, hurling a cooking pot across the room. It missed Jack by a whisker, as he dashed for the door.

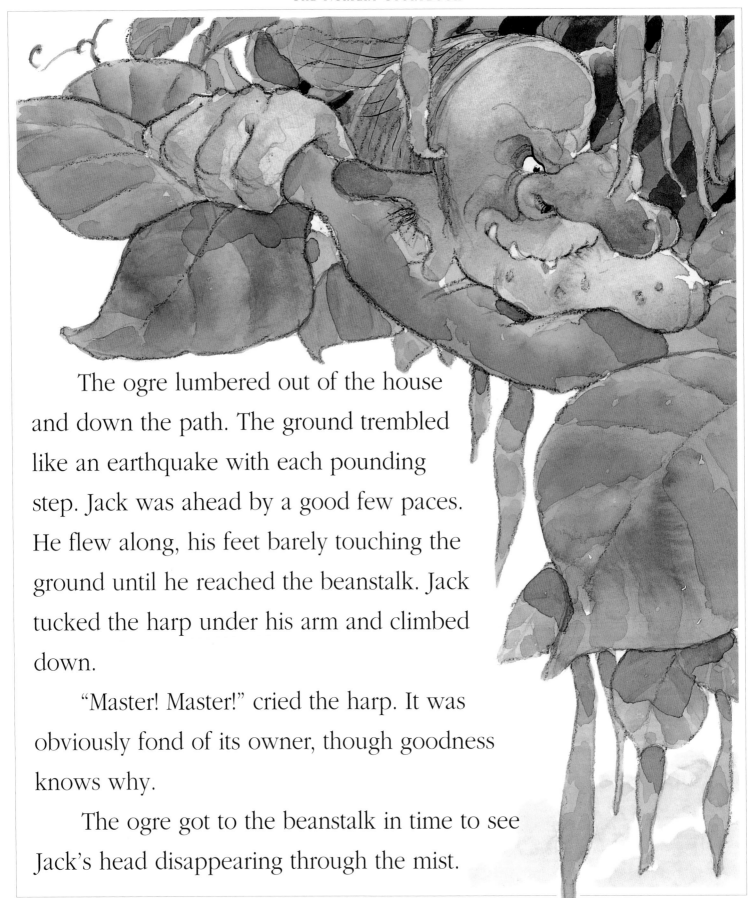

The ogre lumbered out of the house and down the path. The ground trembled like an earthquake with each pounding step. Jack was ahead by a good few paces. He flew along, his feet barely touching the ground until he reached the beanstalk. Jack tucked the harp under his arm and climbed down.

"Master! Master!" cried the harp. It was obviously fond of its owner, though goodness knows why.

The ogre got to the beanstalk in time to see Jack's head disappearing through the mist.

The ogre put one colossal boot on the beanstalk . . .

Jack looked up. He heard the ogre crashing through the leaves. The weight of that blundering brute was shaking the beanstalk from top to bottom.

Jack slid and scrambled down the rest of the way. He leaped off at the bottom and shouted to his mother, "Quick! Bring an axe!"

His bewildered mother came pelting out of the cottage.

"Mercy!" screamed the poor woman when she saw what was going on.

Jack chopped away at the beanstalk, as if his life depended upon it. Which it did. He chopped and chopped and CHOPPED until . . . the beanstalk split in two.

"Watch out, mother!" shouted Jack, as the beanstalk came toppling down. The ogre landed on his head with an ear-splitting *thud*! And that was the end of him.

After that, the harp settled down to play for Jack and his mother. People came from all over the place to listen.

One day, a princess got to hear about Jack's special harp and she came to visit him. She took one look at Jack and fell in love.

So Jack married the princess and became Prince Jack. He took his mother, the hen and the harp to live in the palace, and they all lived happily ever after.